train

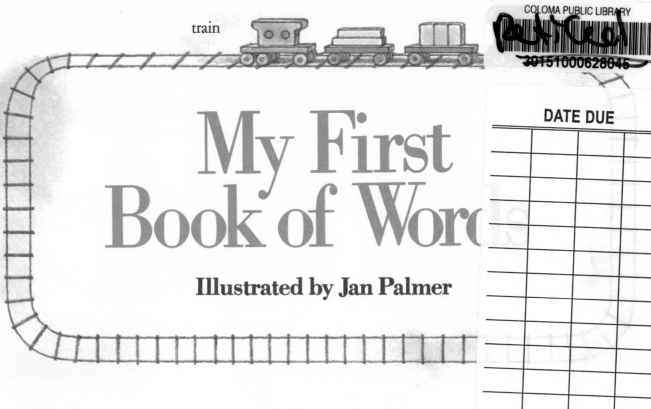

My First Book of Words

Illustrated by Jan Palmer

Golden Press • New York

Western Publishing Company, Inc.
Racine, Wisconsin

bugle

mouse

Words About Me

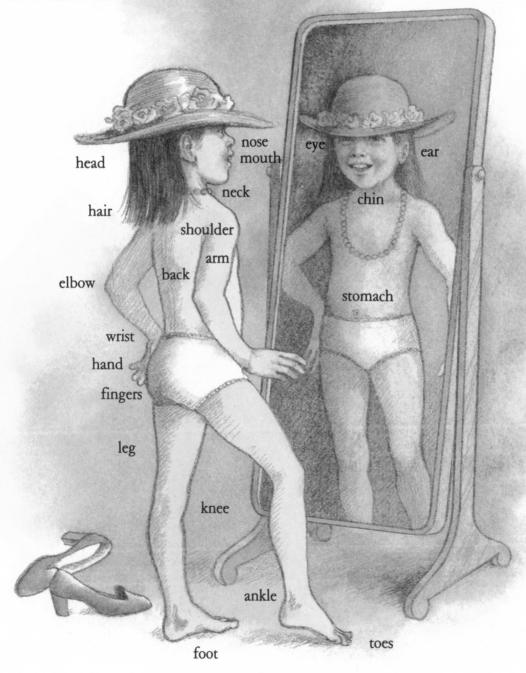

My Family

My House

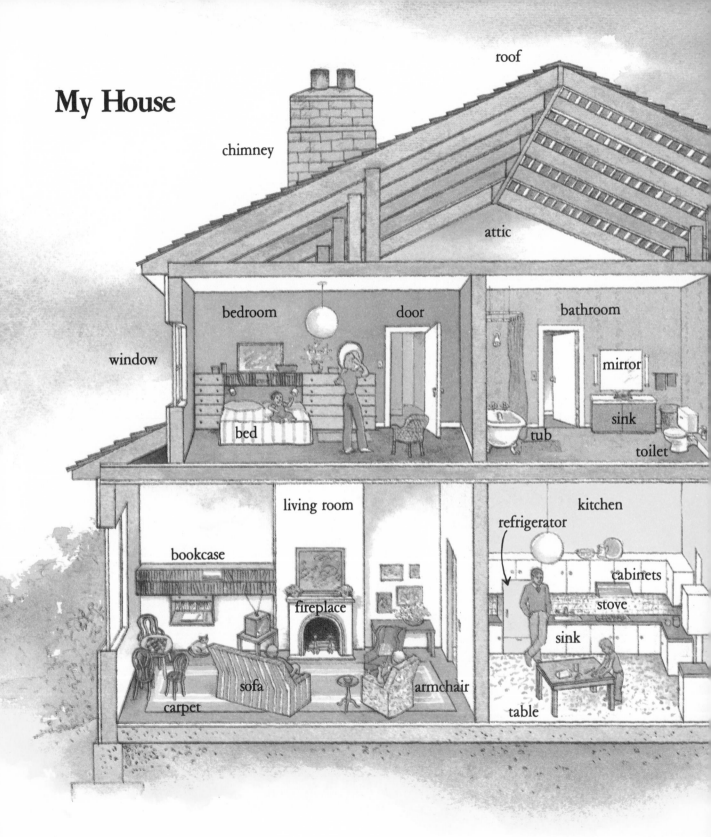

roof

chimney

attic

bedroom

door

bathroom

window

mirror

sink

bed

tub

toilet

living room

kitchen

refrigerator

bookcase

cabinets

stove

fireplace

sink

sofa

armchair

carpet

table

bedroom

tree

bed

tree house

garage

yard

ladder   skis   rake

bicycle

bush

lawn mower

automobile

trash cans

grass

My Room

curtains

seashells

poster

pictures

window

bookcase   books

goldfish
bowl

piggy bank

chest of
drawers

pillow

toy chest

lamp

truck

bedspread

blanket

rug

bed

night table

My Toys

doll

puppet

dollhouse

teddy bear

rocking horse

ball

game

jack-in-the-box

wagon

yo-yo

Foods I Like

Clothes I Wear

rainhat

mitten

baseball cap

sweater

scarf

skirt

belt

coat

overalls

bathing
suit

raincoat

pants

sock

robe

sneaker

boot

pajamas

slipper

gloves

clock

My Classroom

bulletin board

water fountain

globe

calendar

map

pencil
sharpener

desk

piano

wastepaper
basket

cymbals

paper

workbook

ruler   paste

blocks

record player

teacher

alphabet

ABCDEF
GHIJKL
MNOPQR
STUVW
XYZ

lunch box

chalkboard

easel

eraser

brush

chalk

paint

smock

books

crayons

pupils

scissors

hand puppets

chair

modeling clay

table

My Schoolyard

flag

flagpole

school

baseball bat

seesaw

school bus

laughing

somersaulting

falling

hopping

skipping

running

My Town

lighthouse

traffic light

bridge

park

river

harbor

SUPERMARKET

shopping cart

GAS

bench   fountain

LIBRARY

phone booth

sidewalk

barge tugboat sailboat buoy school

church bank

MOVIES

MEAT MARKET HARDWARE DRUGS

street sign

police officer newsstand

fire hydrant stop sign

BARBER SHOP SHOE REPAIR DRY CLEANING FUR STORAGE

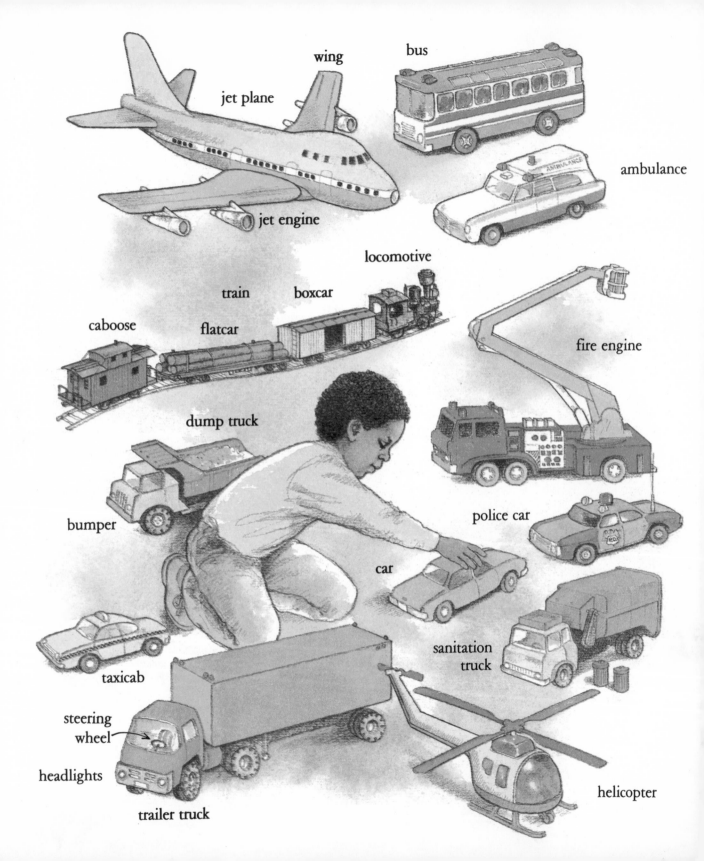

wing

bus

jet plane

jet engine

ambulance

locomotive

train

boxcar

caboose

flatcar

fire engine

dump truck

bumper

police car

car

taxicab

sanitation truck

steering wheel

headlights

helicopter

trailer truck

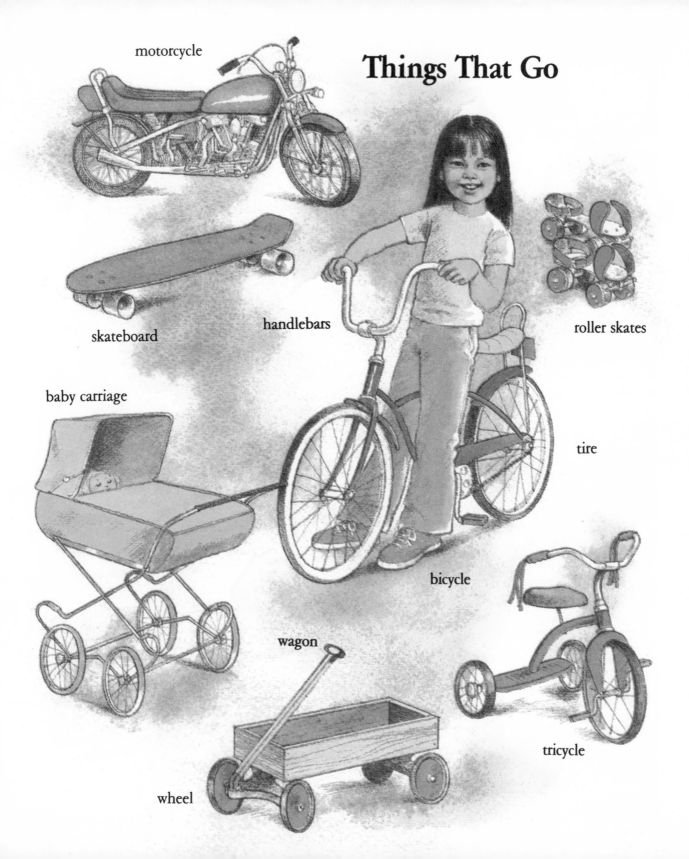

motorcycle

Things That Go

skateboard

handlebars

roller skates

baby carriage

tire

bicycle

wagon

tricycle

wheel

Animals in the Zoo

giraffe

elephant

kangaroo

monkey

lion

seal

snake

ostrich

penguin

bear

Animals on the Farm

cow

horse

donkey

sheep

pig

goat

goose

chicken

rooster

duck

The Seasons

Summer

tree house

rosebush

lawn mower

sprinkler

Fall

jack-o-lantern

book bag

football

rake

leaves